THE NUTCRACKER

Retold and Illustrated by

RACHEL ISADORA

MACMILLAN PUBLISHING CO., INC.
New York
COLLIER MACMILLAN PUBLISHERS
London

For Judy Kohlhaas

Macmillan Publishing Co., Inc.
866 Third Avenue, New York, N.Y. 10022
Collier Macmillan Canada, Ltd.
Printed in the United States of America
10 9 8 7 6 5 4 3 2 1

Library of Congress Cataloging in Publication Data
Isadora, Rachel.
  The nutcracker.

  Adaptation of: Nussknacker und Mausekönig.
  Summary: A little girl travels with the Nutcracker
Prince to the Land of Cake and Candy.

  [1. Fairy tales] I. Hoffman, E. T. A. (Ernst
Theodor Amadeus), 1776-1822. Nussknacker und
Mausekönig. II. Title.
PZ8.I84Nu [E] 81-6042 ISBN 0-02-747470-4 AACR2

It is Christmas Eve and glistening snow falls softly on a small town in Germany. Bright silver bells ring out through the frosty air as horse-drawn sleighs are pulled through the streets to the Silberhaus home. Judge Silberhaus, his wife, and their two children, Clara and Fritz, joyfully greet their guests as the scents of pine needles, cinnamon, and clove-studded apples draw the party to the ballroom. Gaily wrapped gifts are admired and then happily exchanged before the magnificent tree, laden with tiny glass ornaments, golden tinsel, and flickering candles. Suddenly there appears a special guest, Clara's godfather, Doctor Drosselmeyer. It is rumored that he is not an ordinary doctor and that he possesses strange and mysterious powers. He is also a renowned inventor, and tonight his arms are filled with wonderful gifts. To Fritz, he gives a splendid army of small wooden soldiers. For Clara, there is a special surprise.

Doctor Drosselmeyer reaches deep within the folds of his satin cape and slowly withdraws a finely carved Nutcracker. "Oh, thank you, dear Godfather!" says Clara, gently cradling the doll while lightly stroking its soft curly beard.

"Give him to me," Fritz demands, seeing what an excellent leader the Nutcracker will make for his new soldiers. He grabs the Nutcracker from Clara's arms, but as he starts across the room, he trips and drops the Nutcracker to the floor.

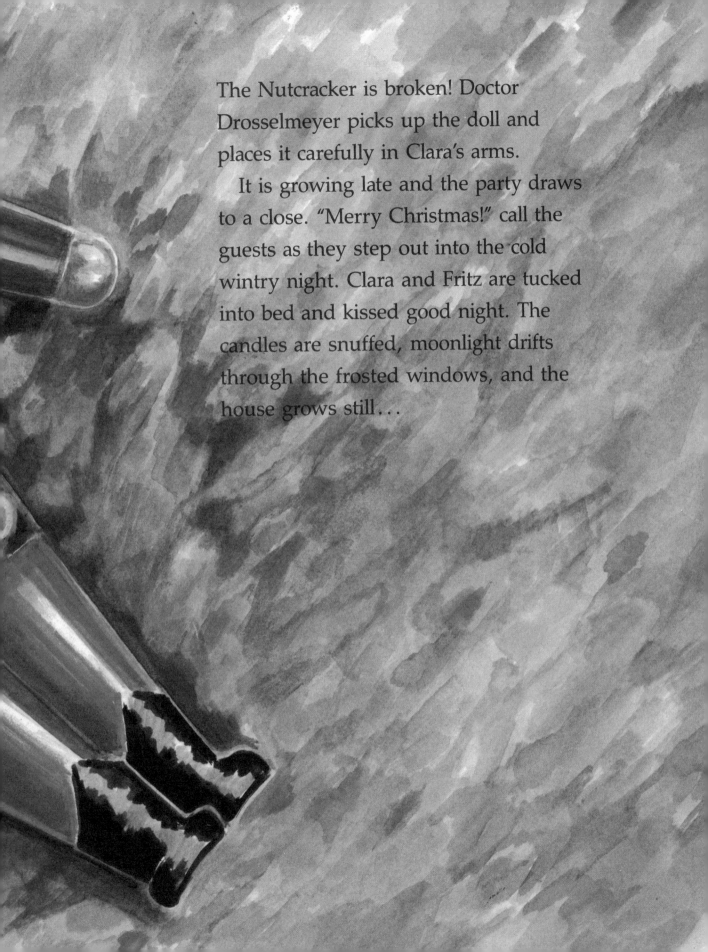

The Nutcracker is broken! Doctor
Drosselmeyer picks up the doll and
places it carefully in Clara's arms.

It is growing late and the party draws
to a close. "Merry Christmas!" call the
guests as they step out into the cold
wintry night. Clara and Fritz are tucked
into bed and kissed good night. The
candles are snuffed, moonlight drifts
through the frosted windows, and the
house grows still...

…except in Clara's room. Deep in the shadows, Doctor Drosselmeyer quietly repairs the broken Nutcracker. When he has finished, he places the doll next to Clara and disappears.

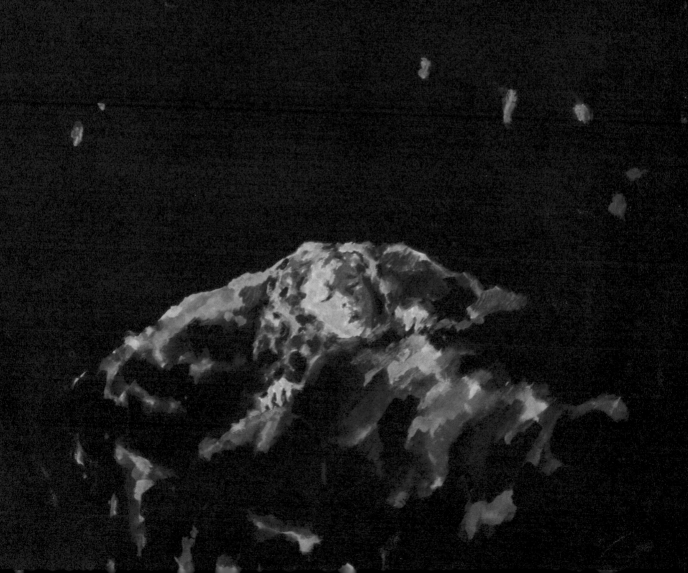

The grandfather clock
strikes twelve and
awakens Clara. She hears a
faint noise and sees her
bedroom window slowly open.

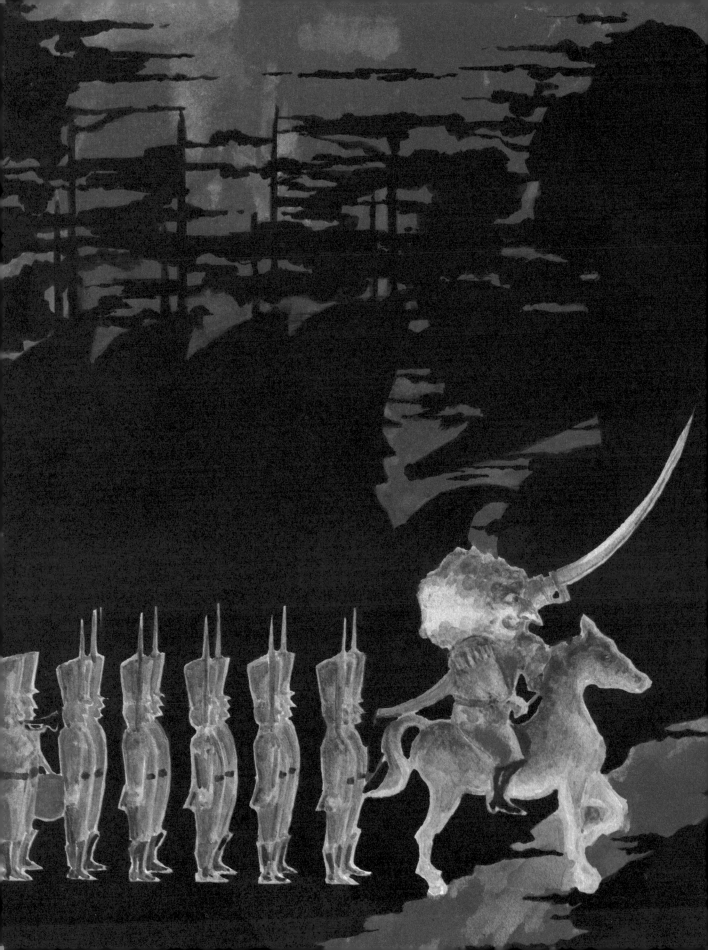

Great gray mice pour into Clara's room,
led by a ferocious mouse with seven
heads—the Mouse King. Suddenly,
the Nutcracker calls in Fritz's
soldiers to lead them into battle.

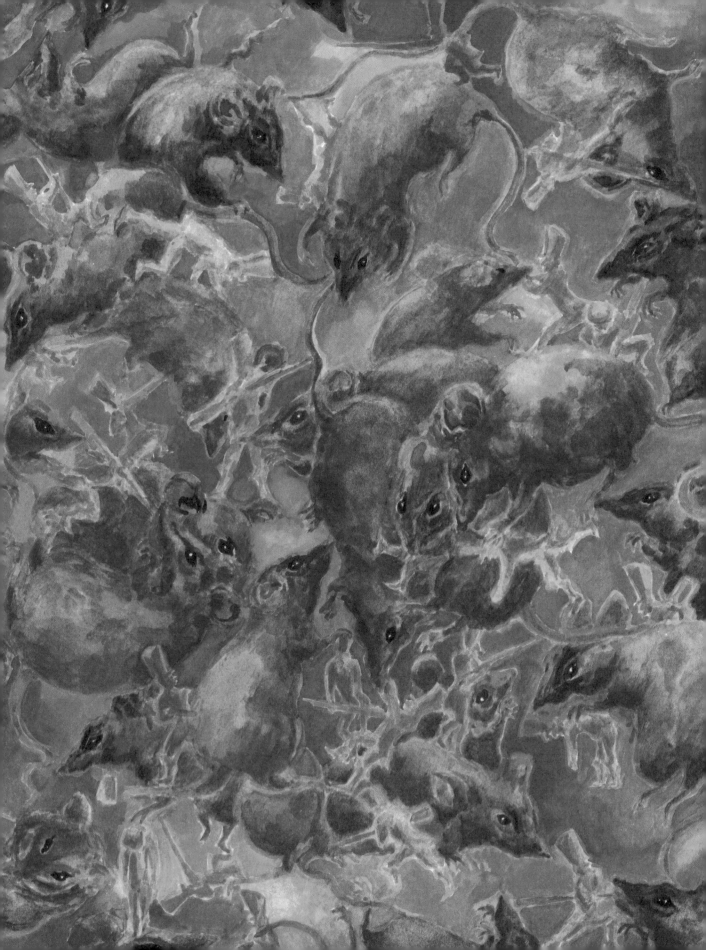

Bayonets flash and hissing fills the air.
Without warning, the Mouse King attacks
the Nutcracker from behind. Clara screams
and pulls the Mouse King's lashing tail. As
the giant mouse turns toward Clara, the
Nutcracker raises his sword and slays the
giant mouse.

The Nutcracker turns and faces Clara.
He is no longer a doll. He is now a
young Prince. He removes a crown from
the Mouse King and places it gently on
Clara's head. "You saved my life," he
says, "and I crown you Princess Clara.
Come! My kingdom is near."

The Prince takes Clara's hand and their journey begins.
Sparkling snow falls about them though it is not cold.

They run through glittering ice crystals
in the Land of Frost.

Soon they come to gates of sparkling spun sugar.
Peppermint sticks line a candy road. The soft
breezes of spring are all about them. "Hurry," says
the Prince. "They are waiting."

At the end of the road stands a glowing castle, made entirely of marzipan. "Welcome," says the Sugar Plum Fairy. "Your kingdom awaits your return." Trumpets sound and music fills the air. The celebration begins.

Clara and the Prince join hands and
dance, and they dance far into the
night. And as they dance their final
waltz, pink and gold clouds flow about
them and the pale sun begins to rise.